HORRiD HENRY'S
Nightmare

Francesca Simon
Illustrated by Tony Ross

Orion
Children's Books

ORION CHILDREN'S BOOKS

First published in Great Britain in 2013 by Orion Children's Books
This edition published in 2016 by Hodder and Stoughton

30

Text copyright © Francesca Simon, 2013
Illustrations copyright © Tony Ross, 2013

The moral rights of the author and illustrator have been asserted.

A CIP catalogue record for this book
is available from the British Library.

ISBN 978 1 4072 4877 6

Printed and bound in Great Britain
by Clays Ltd, Elcograf S.p.A.

The paper and board used in this book are
made from wood from responsible sources.

Orion Children's Books
An imprint of
Hachette Children's Group
Part of Hodder and Stoughton
Carmelite House
50 Victoria Embankment
London EC4Y 0DZ

An Hachette UK Company
www.hachette.co.uk

www.hachettechildrens.co.uk
www.horridhenry.co.uk

For Judith Elliott,
the visionary editor who thought
Horrid Henry might work

CONTENTS

1

HORRID HENRY'S NIGHTMARE

". . . and then the slime-covered, flesh-eating zombie, fangs dripping blood, lurched into school, wailing and gnashing and – pouncing!" screamed Rude Ralph, grabbing Horrid Henry.

Henry shrieked.

"Ha ha, gotcha," said Ralph.

Horrid Henry's heart pounded. How he loved being scared! What could be better than having a sleepover with Ralph, and both of them trying to scare the other? He reached into the Purple Hand Fort's top secret skull and bones biscuit tin, and scoffed a big handful of chocolate gooey chewies. Scary stories and chocolate. Whoopie!

"Watch out, Ralph," said Henry. "I'm gonna tell you about the alien acid monster who creeps—"

"Smelly toads," piped a little voice outside the Purple Hand Fort.

Grrr.

"Hide," hissed Horrid Henry.

Rude Ralph belched.

"I know you're in there, Henry," said Peter.

2

"No I'm not," said Henry.

"And I said the password, so you have to let me in," said Peter. "It's my fort too. Mum said so."

Horrid Henry sighed loudly. Why on earth, of all the possible brothers in the world, did he have to get stuck with Peter? Why oh why, when younger brothers were being distributed, did he get landed with a tell-tale, smelly nappy baby?

"All right, come in," said Henry.

Perfect Peter crept through the branches.

"Why is it so dark in here?" said Peter.

"None of your business, baby," said Henry. "You've been in, now get out."

"Yeah, wriggle off, worm," said Ralph.

"No babies allowed in the Purple Hand Fort," said Henry.

Perfect Peter stuck out his lower lip. "I'm going to tell Mum you wouldn't let me stay in the fort. And that you called me a baby."

"Go ahead, baby boo boo," said Henry.

"MUM!" screamed Peter. "Henry called me baby boo boo."

"Stop being horrid, Henry, and be nice to your brother," shouted Mum. "Or I'll send Ralph home."

"I wasn't being horrid," bellowed Henry. Oh to be a wizard and turn Peter into a toadstool.

"Okay, Peter, you can stay," snarled Henry. "But you'll be sorry."

"No I won't," said Peter.

"We're telling scary stories," said Ralph.

"And you hate scary stories," said Henry.

Peter considered. It was true, he hated being scared. And almost everything scared him. But maybe that was last week. Maybe now that he was a week older he wouldn't be scared any more.

"I'm brave now," said Peter.

Horrid Henry shrugged. "Well, just don't blame me when you wake up screaming tonight," he shrieked.

Peter jumped. Should he stay and listen to these terrible tales? Then he squared his shoulders. He wasn't a baby, whatever Henry said. He was a big boy.

Horrid Henry
told his scariest
story about the
child-eating
vampire werewolf.
Rude Ralph told
his scariest story
about the wailing
graveyard ghost
who slurped up
babies. Then Henry
told his most scary
story ever in the
history of the
world: the alien
acid monster and
zombie mummy
who—

"I know a scary
story," interrupted
Peter.

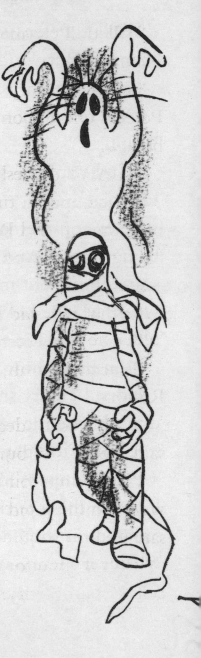

"We don't want to hear it," said Henry.

"It's really scary, I promise," said Peter. "Once upon a time there was a bunny . . ."

"SCARY stories!" shouted Rude Ralph.

"Once upon a time there was a really big bunny," said Peter. "And one day his little tail fell off."

Peter paused.

"Is that it?" said Henry.

"Yes," said Peter.

"Blecccccchhhh," belched Rude Ralph.

"That's your idea of a scary story?" said Henry. "A bunny with no tail?"

"Wouldn't you be scared if you were a bunny and your tail fell off?" said Peter.

"Isn't it time for you to practise your cello?" said Henry.

Peter gasped.

He didn't ever like to miss a day's practice.

Perfect Peter trotted off.

Phew. Worm-free at last.

"Now, as I was telling you, Ralph," said Horrid Henry, "there was once a zombie mummy that roamed . . ."

NO!!!!!

Horrid Henry lay in bed in his dark bedroom, trembling. What a horrible, horrible nightmare. All about a ghost bunny with huge teeth and no tail, charging at him waving a gigantic needle. Ugggh. His heart was pounding so fast he thought it would pop out of his chest.

But what to do, what to do?

Henry was too scared to stay in bed. Henry was too scared to move. Don't

be an idiot, snarled Devil 1. There is no such thing as a ghost bunny. Yeah, you lummox, snarled Devil 2. What a wimp. Frankly, I'm disappointed.

9

But Horrid Henry was too terrified to listen to reason. What if that alien acid monster or the ghost bunny was hiding under his bed? Horrid Henry wanted to lean over and check, but he couldn't. Because what if the wailing graveyard ghost had sneaked into his wardrobe and was just waiting to GRAB him?

Worst of all, there was Ralph, snoring happily away in his sleeping bag. How could he just lie there when he was going to get gobbled up any second?

"Ralph," hissed Henry.

"Shut up," mumbled Ralph, rudely.

"I'm . . ." But what could Horrid Henry say? If he told Ralph he was — Horrid Henry could barely even think the word — scared, he'd never hear the end of it. Everyone would call him,

Henry, leader of the Purple Hand Gang,
a goochy goochy nappy baby.

Yikes.

Should he stay in bed and get eaten by
the alien acid monster, or get out of bed
and get eaten by the wailing graveyard
ghost?

Actually, thought Horrid Henry, the
acid monster would get Ralph first,
since he was asleep on the floor. But if
he jumped really fast, he could race out
the door and down the hall to Mum and
Dad's room before the graveyard ghost
could grab him.

But should he leave
Ralph alone to face the
monsters?

Yes! thought Horrid
Henry, leaping out of bed
and trampling on Rude
Ralph's head.

11

"Uhhh," groaned Ralph. "Watch where you're going, you big fat . . ."

But Horrid Henry wasn't listening. He stampeded to the bedroom door, dashed into the dark hallway and slammed the door behind him. Right now he was so scared he didn't care if he was too old to jump into Mum and Dad's bed.

Phew. Horrid Henry paused, gasping for breath.

He was safe. The
monsters would be
too busy chomping on
Ralph to nab him.

But wait. Could the
graveyard ghost ooze under the door
and grab him in the hall? Worse, was
the injection bunny gliding up the stairs?

Horrid Henry froze. Oh no. His heart
was pounding.

He opened his mouth to shriek
"MUM!"

Then he closed it.

Wait a minute. Wait a minute.

Peter was sure to be awake, after
all the horrible scary stories he'd
heard today. After all, Peter
was the biggest scaredy-
cat ever. If Henry was
scared, Peter would be
a dripping wreck.

He'd just drop in. Seeing Peter
terrified would make him feel a whole
lot better, and a whole lot braver.

I'll bet Peter's lying there shaking and
too scared to move, thought Horrid
Henry. Ha. Ha. Ha.

Horrid Henry crept into Peter's room
and shut the door. Then he tip-toed
over to Peter's bed . . .

Huh?

There was Peter, sound asleep, a
sweet smile on his face, his peaceful
face lit up by his bunny nightlight and
ceiling stars.

Horrid Henry's jaw dropped. How
could Peter not be having horrible
nightmares too? It was so unfair! He was
the brave one, scared of nothing (except
injections) and Peter was the wormy
worm wibble pants noodle-head who
was scared of Rudy the Rootin-Tootin

Rooster cartoon, Santa Claus, and probably the Tooth Fairy.

Well, he'd do something about that.

"Slimy acid monster," murmured Henry in Peter's ear. "Coming to get you with his great big googly eyes and great big monster teeth. Be afraid, Peter. Be very afraid. OOOOOOOOOOOOOHHH."

15

Perfect Peter smiled
in his sleep.

"Hello Mr
Monster," he
said.

"BOO!" said
Horrid Henry.
"BOOO!"

"Would
you like a
cup of tea?"
murmured
Peter.

"No," growled Horrid Henry. "I want
to eat YOU!"

"Okay," said Peter drowsily.

What was wrong with him? thought
Horrid Henry.

"Mwaahahahahahaha," cackled Horrid
Henry. "I'm the graveyard ghost come to
GET ya."

"That's nice,"
murmured
Peter.

"No, it's not
nice," growled
Horrid Henry.
"It's scary.
It's terrible.
Woooooooooo!
Arrrrggghhhhh!
**BOOOOOO-
OOOOO-
OOO!**"

Suddenly Peter's
door opened.

"AAAAAAAARRRRGGGHHH!"
screamed Horrid Henry.

"AAAAAAAARRRRGGGHHH!"
screamed Perfect Peter.

"What are you doing in here, Henry?"
said Mum.

"It's 3 o'clock in the morning," said
Dad.

Horrid Henry was never so happy to
see anyone in his life.

"I thought Peter would be scared, so I
came in to check on him," said Horrid
Henry.

Mum stared at Henry.

"And why did you think Peter would
be scared?" asked Mum. She looked
suspiciously at Henry.

18

"'Cause I just did," said Henry.

"Go back to your room, Henry," said Mum.

His room? His haunted horrible room where all the monsters were lurking?

"Mum, could you just come with me?" said Henry. "I need you to check on something."

"Can't it wait till morning?" said Dad, yawning.

"No," said Horrid Henry. "I think there's a tarantula under my bed. Could you check please?"

After all, if Mum saw an acid alien there instead of a tarantula, she'd probably mention it.

Mum sighed, walked him to his room and checked under the bed.

"There's nothing there," said Mum.

"Oh, and in my wardrobe, I'm sure I saw a . . . umm . . . mouse run in," said Henry. "That's what woke me. Could you just check for me?"

Mum looked in the wardrobe.

"That's it, Henry," snapped Mum. "Now go to sleep."

Horrid Henry climbed back into bed and sighed happily. His room looked just as friendly and familiar as usual.

Why on earth had he been scared?

"Pssst, Ralph, you awake?" hissed Henry.

"Yeah," said Rude Ralph, sitting up.

"Wanna hear a scary story?" said Henry. "I know a great one about

20

a mouldering monster and a cursed
monkey paw . . ."

"Yeah!" said Rude Ralph.

2

HORRID HENRY AND THE REVENGE OF THE DEMON DINNER LADY

Horrid Henry crumpled up the paper and took aim. There was the back of Margaret's head, so temptingly displayed in front of him. Tee hee. Wouldn't she get a shock when a big wet spitball splatted her—

THWACK!

A dripping spitball whacked Horrid Henry on the neck. He turned round, glaring.

Who had dared to spitball him
during assembly? Rude Ralph was
snickering. But so were Dizzy Dave
and Brainy Brian. Well, just wait. Just
wait. When he got his hands on—

"Settle down. Settle down, please,"
barked Mrs Oddbod. "Henry. Turn
round and face the front. I have some
important announcements."

Horrid Henry scowled. What could
be more important than finding out
who had spitballed him? That the
infants would be practising their barn
dance at playtime? That Perfect Peter
was in the Good as Gold Book again?
That Miss Battle-Axe was joining the
circus? Now that, thought Horrid
Henry, would be an announcement
worth hearing. Anything else – big
fat yawn.

Mrs Oddbod gabbled on. "As you all

know, this school is dedicated to healthy eating."

Oh no, not another lecture, thought Horrid Henry. If he heard the horrible words *vegetables*, *fruit* and *wholemeal bread* again he would scream.

"However" – she glared at Greedy Graham, Horrid Henry, and Rude Ralph – "some of you appear not to know the meaning of the word *healthy*. Some of you keep bringing packed lunches to school filled with unhealthy, sugary snacks.

25

A bar of chocolate is not
a healthy meal."

Yummy, thought Horrid Henry.
Three of his favourite words. Sugar.
Snacks. Chocolate. He'd sneaked two
bags of Pickled Onion Monster Munch
into his Mutant Max lunchbox when
Dad's back was turned. And he'd traded
Bert an egg and cress sandwich for
some Chocolate Crunchy Crackles.
Hmmm, boy, was he looking forward to
lunchtime. He was sure he could pinch
a pack of Super Spicy Hedgehog crisps
from William when he was crying about
something or other. And swap his raisins
for Greedy Graham's chocolate fudge
bars. What a feast awaited him.

"Good job, Henry," burped his belly.
"You sure know how to look after me."

"We've decided to appoint a lunchbox
monitor, who will be checking every

day and confiscating
all unhealthy snacks,"
said Mrs Oddbod.
"From today we
will be a sweet-free
school."

Huh?

Horrid Henry sat
up. This did not
sound good. In
fact, this sounded
TERRIBLE.

"I'm delighted to
welcome back an old
friend to our school,
someone who has
been sorely missed.
Children, please say
hello to our new
healthy food monitor
– Greta!"

27

An enormous woman stood up and waddled over to Mrs Oddbod. Horrid Henry's blood turned to ice. It wasn't – it couldn't be—

Greta. Greasy Greta. Greasy Greta, the Demon Dinner Lady! That ape in an apron, that demon in dungarees, that sneaky sweet-snatcher, that gobbling treat-grabber. The last time Henry had seen Greta she'd run howling out of school after he'd spiked some biscuits with hot chilli powder. And now she was back . . . bigger and meaner and more demonic than ever.

Greasy Greta, a healthy food monitor? She'd grab all the treats for herself, and leave the carrots and celery sticks and wholemeal bread behind. No one could sniff out sweets faster than Greasy Greta.

"I'll be checking all lunchboxes *very* thoroughly," said Greasy Greta. "Very

28

very thoroughly. No sneaky sweets will escape *me*."

"Are there any questions?" said Mrs Oddbod.

Greedy Graham's hand shot up.

"What's going to happen to all the sweets?" he asked.

29

"All confiscated sweets will be given to charity," said Mrs Oddbod.

"That's right," said Greta. "All confiscated sweets will be safely disposed of." And she smiled her horrible greasy smile and flashed her mouldy teeth.

Yeah, down her gob, thought Horrid Henry mournfully. What a job. Like putting a fox in charge of the rabbit hutches.

"Greta will also be giving healthy-eating talks," said Mrs Oddbod.

"Sweets are bad for you," said Greta. "I never touch them. Eat vegetables."

What a liar, thought Horrid Henry. I'll bet she's never eaten a vegetable in her life.

But what to do? What to do? He couldn't face school lunches with Sloppy Sally sloshing food all over his tray. He wanted to keep his packed lunch AND all his treats. But how? How? Somehow he'd have to find a way . . .

Snatch. Crunch Crunch.

   Snatch. Chomp Chomp.

Snatch. Gobble Gobble.

There was the rumbling, grumbling sound of a dinosaur approaching. Glasses shook. Trays trembled. Cutlery rattled. Wobbling and gobbling, Greasy Greta was on patrol.

"Gimme that lunchbox," she thundered.

Greedy Graham flung his arms around his lunchbox, but he was no match for Greasy Greta.

Snatch! Pop!

Greedy Graham's lunchbox popped open. Greasy Greta emptied all the sweets and fizzy drinks into her gigantic pockets.

"Next!" she bellowed.

Norwegian Norris tried to hide his treats in his pockets, but Greasy Greta's X-ray eyes spotted them.

"Hand them over," she barked, holding out her apron pockets.

"No," said Norwegian Norris.

"GIMME YOUR SWEETS!" roared
Greta.

Norwegian Norris obeyed.

"This wouldn't happen in Norway,"
he wailed.

Next up for inspection was Horrid
Henry.

Greta towered over him.

"Open your lunchbox," she ordered.

Henry opened the lid.

She'll never find *my*
sweets, thought
Horrid Henry.
He'd tucked his
chocolate fudge
bars up his
sleeves, leaving
the carrot sticks
that he would be
trading as soon as
he escaped.

Ha, ha, she'd never ever— Before he could even finish that thought Greta snatched his sleeves and shook out his sweets into her bulging pockets.

She was a bloodhound.

Next up was Pasty Patsy. She beamed at Greasy Greta. Greasy Greta beamed at her.

"Run along, dear," said Greasy Greta.

Huh?

"How come you didn't get inspected?" said Henry.

Pasty Patsy tossed her stringy hair and puffed out her marshmallow cheeks.

"'Cause she's my mum," said Pasty Patsy. "I can have anything I like for lunch."

Patsy snapped open her lunchbox, displaying rows and rows of sweets. Then she grabbed a handful and gulped them down.

"Nah na ne nah nah," smirked Pasty Patsy.

Horrid Henry's mouth watered.

It was so unfair.

"Mum," said Henry that evening, "the Demon Dinner Lady is back and she's snatching our sweets."

"Good," said Mum. "You're not allowed to take sweets to school any more."

"But she's supposed to be the healthy-eating monitor and she's eating all the sweets herself."

"Glad to hear it," said Dad.

"It's not fair," wailed Henry.

Why did he have such mean, horrible parents? How could he live in a world with no sweets in school? He'd die. He'd shrivel up into a little bit of thread and be blown away by the wind. He'd never be able to learn anything again, as all he'd be thinking about was sweets. He was doomed forever to a lunchbox of celery sticks and carrots and brown bread sandwiches with crusts.

Oh, woe woe woe.

And then suddenly Horrid Henry had a brilliant, spectacular idea. It was so brilliant, and so spectacular, and yet so simple, that for a moment he could scarcely breathe. He would set up in business. The sweet-selling business. Who better than Horrid Henry to ride to the rescue of all his poor, starving, suffering schoolmates whose mean, horrible parents were obeying the new no-sweets rule? He'd buy up loads of chocolates on his way to school, then sell them for twice the price in the morning break.

He'd be rich!

Business was brisk. Word spread through the playground that Horrid Henry's top secret sweet shop was open in the Nature Reserve behind the climbing frame. Soon everyone's mouths were bulging with sweets and treats, and Horrid Henry's pockets were bulging with cash. At this rate he'd be a billionaire, thought Horrid Henry happily. No, a trillionaire. No, a gazillionaire. And so long as everyone

38

scoffed their sweets before Greta's inspection,
she'd be left empty-handed. The Demon
Dinner Lady would be defeated!

Tra-La-La. Horrid Henry sat
on the bench counting his
cash before the bell rang.

Oh, the lovely, lovely sweets. Oh, the
lovely, lovely money. Tomorrow he'd
buy even more—

A dark, hideous shadow fell across him.

Oh no. Help! Greasy Greta had sniffed him out.

Horrid Henry looked up, trying to hide all the unsold sweets filling his lap.

But it *wasn't* the Demon Dinner Lady. It was the head teacher, Mrs Oddbod. She was on the warpath.

"Henry," she said. "Stand up at once."

Uh oh.

"How could you do this, Henry?" said Mrs Oddbod. "You know there are no sweets allowed in school."

"There aren't?" said Henry, trying to look as innocent as possible.

"Come with me. Those sweets will go straight into our charity cupboard."

"But . . . but . . ." spluttered Horrid Henry.

"No buts, you know the rules," said Mrs Oddbod.

Horrid Henry wanted to scream. All his supplies. His lovely shop. His sweet-selling business, closed down before he'd made his first million.

Mrs Oddbod marched Horrid Henry down the hallway to the large storage cupboard. Every step spelled doom. Oh, my lovely chocolates, moaned Horrid Henry. Oh, my lovely money.

And he was in trouble. Big, big trouble.

"I am so disappointed in you, bringing sweets to school," said Mrs Oddbod, unlocking the cupboard. "And after all Greta's hard work, collecting sweets for charity," she added, flinging open the door, "I just don't know how you could—"

Greasy Greta stood in the cupboard buried in sweets. Her face was smeared with chocolate. So were her hands. Sweet wrappers piled up around her.

"Greta!" shrieked Mrs Oddbod. "Is this how you set an example of healthy eating?"

Greta's great fish mouth gaped open. And then closed. She leapt out of the cupboard and pounded down the hall, scattering sweets everywhere.

"You're fired!" shouted Mrs Oddbod after her.

Could those be the loveliest words Horrid Henry had ever heard?

"That's what I was trying to tell you," said Horrid Henry. "I collected those sweets for charity and I was trying to hide them from her in the Nature Reserve when you found me. I knew she'd just eat them. You saw her."

That *wasn't* a lie. He was trying to hide the sweets from Greta. And the sweets *were* for his favourite charity, *Child in Need*. He was a child, and he was in need, so it was right that he benefit.

"Hmmmm," said Mrs Oddbod. "Hmmmm. Well then Henry, perhaps *you* would like to be the new healthy food monitor?"

"Me?" said Horrid Henry.

"You," said Mrs Oddbod.

Horrid Henry could not believe his ears. He'd never have to buy sweets again.

"Me inspect lunchboxes for sweets? I'd love to. I know all the hiding places, I can—"

"No," said Mrs Oddbod. "You'll lead by example. Only healthy food in your lunchbox from now on. Or else." She glared at him.

"Oh," said Horrid Henry. "Rats."
Goodbye chocolate, crisps and sweets.
Hello wholemeal bread and carrot sticks.
Wah.

3

....

FLUFFY STRUTS
HER STUFF

"Fluffy. Fetch," said Perfect Peter.

Snore.

"Fluffy. Fetch!" said Perfect Peter.

Snore.

"Go on, Fluffy," said Perfect Peter,
dangling a squeaky toy tarantula in front
of the snoozing cat. "Fetch!"

Fat Fluffy stretched.

Yawn.

Snore. Snore.

"What *are* you doing, worm?" said
Horrid Henry.

Peter jumped. Should he tell Henry
about his brilliant idea? What if
Henry copied him? That
would be just like Henry.
Well, let him try, thought
Peter. Fluffy is my cat.

"I'm training Fluffy for
Scruffs," said Peter. "She's
sure to win this year."

Scruffs was the annual
neighbourhood pet
show. Last year Henry
had spent one of the
most boring days of his
life watching horrible
dogs compete for who looked the
most like their owner, or who had the
waggiest tail or fluffiest coat.

Horrid Henry snorted.

48

"Which category?" said
Henry. "Ugliest Owner?
Fattest Cat?"

"*Most Obedient*,"
said Peter.

Horrid Henry
snorted again.
Trust his worm
toad nappy face brother to
come up with such
a dumb idea.

Fat Fluffy was the
world's most useless cat.
Fluffy did nothing
but eat and
sleep and
snore. She
was so lazy that
Horrid Henry was
shocked every time
she moved.

Squeak! Perfect Peter waved the
rubber tarantula in front of Fluffy's
face. He knew Henry would make fun
of him. Well, this time he, Peter, would
have the last laugh. He would show the
world what an amazing cat Fluffy was,
and no one, especially Henry,
could stop him. Peter knew that
Fluffy had hidden greatness.
After all, thought Peter, not
everyone knows how clever
I am. The same was true of Fluffy.

"Fluffy, when I squeak this toy, you sit
up and give me your paw," said Peter.
"When I squeak it twice, you roll over."

"You can't train a cat,
toad," said Henry.

"Yes I can," said
Peter. "And don't
call me toad." What
did Henry know,

anyway? Nothing. Peter had seen dogs herding sheep. Jumping through hoops. Even dancing.

True, they had all been dogs, and Fluffy was a cat. But she was no ordinary cat.

Horrid Henry smirked.

"Okay Peter, because I'm such a nice brother I'll show you how to train Fluffy," said Henry.

"Can you really?" said Peter.

"Yup," said Henry. "When I give the command, Fluffy will do exactly what I say."

So far that was more than Peter had managed. A lot more.

"And it will only cost you £1," said Henry.

Well, it was definitely worth a pound if it meant Fluffy could win Most Obedient.

Peter handed over the money.

"Now watch and learn, worm," said
Horrid Henry. "Fluffy. Sleep!"

Fluffy slept.

"See?" said Henry. "She obeyed."

Perfect Peter was outraged.

"That doesn't count," said Peter.
"I want my money back."

"You can't have it," said Henry.
"I did exactly what I said I would
do."

"Mum!" wailed Peter. "Henry tricked
me."

"Shut up, toad," said Horrid Henry.

"Mum! Henry told me to shut up,"
screamed Peter.

"Henry! Don't be horrid," shouted
Mum.

Horrid Henry wasn't listening. He
was an idiot. He had just had the most
brilliant, spectacular idea. He could train
Fluffy *and* play the best ever trick on

Peter in the history of the world. No, the universe. That would pay Peter back for getting Henry into such big trouble over breaking Mum's camera. One day, thought Horrid Henry, he would write a famous book collecting all his best tricks, and sell it for a million pounds a copy. Parliament would declare a special holiday – *Henry Day* – to celebrate his brilliance. There would be street parties

and parades in his honour. The Queen
would knight him. But until then . . .
he had work to do.

Horrid Henry gave Peter back his
£1 coin.

Perfect Peter was amazed. Henry
never handed back money voluntarily.
He looked at the coin suspiciously. Had
Henry substituted a plastic pound coin
like the last time?

"That was just a joke," said Henry
smoothly. "Of course I can train Fluffy
for you."

"How?" said Peter. He'd been trying
for days.

"That's my secret," said Henry. "But
I am so confident I can do it I'll even
give you a money-back guarantee."

A money-back guarantee! That
sounded almost too good to be true.
In fact . . .

"Is this a trick?" said Peter.

"No!" said Henry. "Out of the goodness of my heart, I offer to spend my valuable time training your cat. I'm insulted. Just for that I won't—"

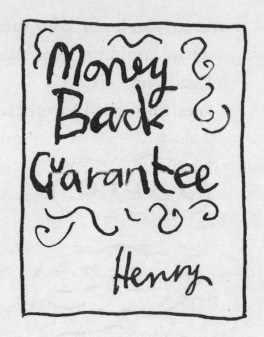

"Okay," said Peter. "How much?"

Yes! thought Horrid Henry.

"£5," said Henry.

"£5!" gasped Peter.

"That's a bargain," said Henry, "Not everyone can train a cat. Okay, £5 money-back guarantee that Fluffy will obey four commands in time for Scruffs.

If not, you'll get your money back."

How could he lose? thought Peter. "Deal," he said.

Yes! thought Horrid Henry.

Somehow he didn't think he'd have too much trouble training Fluffy to Stay. Sleep. Breathe. Snore. No trouble at all.

Perfect Peter bounced up and down with

excitement. Today was the big day.
Today was the day when he took Fluffy
to win Most Obedient pet at Scruffs.

"Shouldn't I practise with her?" said
Peter.

"No!" said Henry quickly. "Cats are
tricky. You only get one chance to
make them obey, so we need to save it
for the judge."

"Okay, Henry," said Peter. After all,
Henry had given him a money-back
guarantee.

Greedy Graham was at the park with
his enormous guinea pig,
Fattie. Rude Ralph
had brought his
mutt, Windbag,
who was
competing for
Waggiest Tail.

Sour Susan was there with her pug, Grumpy. Aerobic Al was there with his greyhound, Speedy. Lazy Linda's rabbit, Snore, dozed on her shoulder. Even Miss Lovely had

brought her Yorkie, Baby Jane. There were pets everywhere.

"What's your dog called, Bert?" said Henry.

"I dunno," said Beefy Bert.

"Waaah," wailed Weepy William. "Mr Socks didn't win the Fluffiest Kitty contest."

"Piddle. Sit!" came a familiar, steely voice, like a jagged knife being dragged across a boulder.

Horrid Henry gasped.

There was Miss Battle-Axe, walking beside the most groomed dog Henry had ever seen. The poodle was covered in ribbons and fancy collars and velvet bows.

He watched as Miss Battle-Axe found a quiet corner and put on some music.

Boom-chick boom-chick boom-chick-boom!

Miss Battle-Axe danced around Piddle.

She clicked her fingers.

Piddle danced around Miss Battle-Axe.

Miss Battle-Axe danced backwards, waving her arms and clicking again.

Piddle danced backwards.

Miss Battle-Axe danced forwards, hopping. Piddle danced forwards.

Double click. Miss Battle-Axe danced off to the left. Piddle danced off to the right. Then they met back at the centre.

Finally, Miss Battle-Axe crouched, and
Piddle jumped over her.

"Wow," said Perfect Peter, glancing
at Fat Fluffy snoring on the grass.
"Do you think we could
teach Fluffy to do tricks
like that?"

"Already have," said Horrid Henry.
Peter gazed at Henry open-mouthed.
"Really?" said Peter.
"Yup," said Henry. "Just squeeze the
tarantula and tell Fluffy what you want
her to do."

"Line up here for Most Obedient pet," said the organiser.

"That's me!" said Peter.

"All you have to remember, one squeak to make Fluffy sit up, two squeaks to make her walk on her hind legs," said Henry as they stood in the queue. "Three squeaks will make her come running to you."

"Okay, Henry," said Peter.

Tee hee.

Revenge was sweet, thought Horrid Henry. Wouldn't Peter look an idiot trying to give orders to a cat? And naturally he'd find a way to keep Peter's £5.

Peter handed in his entry ticket at the enclosure's entrance.

"Sorry, your brother's too young," said the man at the gate. "You'll have to show the cat."

Horrid Henry froze with horror.

"Me?" said Horrid Henry. "But . . . but . . . "

"But she's my cat," said Perfect Peter. "I—"

"Come along, come along, we're about to start," said the man, shoving Henry and Fat Fluffy into the ring.

Horrid Henry found himself standing in the centre. He had the only cat. Everyone was staring and pointing and laughing. Oh, where was a cloak of invisibility when you needed one?

"Put your pets through their paces now," shouted the judge.

All the dogs started to Sit. Stay. Come. Fetch. Piddle the poodle began to dance.

Fluffy lay curled in a ball at Henry's feet.

"Stay!" said Horrid Henry as the judge walked by.

Maybe he could get Fluffy at least to sit up. Or even just move a bit.

Horrid Henry squeezed the tarantula toy.

ZZZZZ

Squeak! "Come on, Fluffy. Move!"

Fluffy didn't even raise her

head.

Squeak! Squeak! Squeak!

"Fluffy. Wake up!"

Aerobic Al's dog began
to bark.

Horrid Henry squeezed the tarantula
toy again.

Squeak! Squeak!

Piddle stood on his hind legs and
danced in a circle.

65

"No, Piddle," hissed Miss Battle-Axe, gesturing wildly, "turn to the right."

"Fluffy. Sit!" said Horrid Henry.

Squeak! Squeak!

Babbling Bob's mutt started growling.

Come on, Fluffy, thought Horrid Henry desperately, squeezing the toy in front of the dozing cat. "Do something. Anything."

Squeeeeeak. Squeeeeeeak! Squeeeeeeeeeeak!

Piddle ran over and peed on the judge's leg.

"Piddle," squawked Miss Battle-Axe. "NO!"

Squeak! Squeak! Squeak!

Sour Susan's dog Grumpy bit the dog next to him.

Horrid Henry waved his arms. "Come on, Fluffy. You can do it!"

Weepy William's dog started running
in circles.

"Piddle! Come back!" shrieked Miss
Battle-Axe as Piddle ran from the ring,

howling. Every
other dog chased
after him, barking
and yelping, their
owners running after
them screaming.

The only animal left
was Fat Fluffy.

"Fluffy. Stay!"
ordered Horrid Henry.

Snore.
Snore. Snore.

"The cat's the
winner," said the
judge.

"Yippee!" screamed Perfect
Peter. "I knew you
could do it, Fluffy!"

"Meow."

4

HORRID HENRY'S MOTHER'S DAY

"What are you doing for Mother's Day?" asked Perfect Peter.

Horrid Henry ignored him and continued to read his *Screamin' Demon* comic.

"I'm getting Mum flowers *and* chocolates *and* making her breakfast in bed," said Peter.

Horrid Henry scowled and slumped lower on the sofa.

"What presents are *you* getting her, Henry?" asked Peter.

"None!" bellowed Horrid Henry. "Now shut up and go away."

"Dad!" wailed Peter. "Henry told me to shut up."

"Don't be horrid, Henry," said Dad. "Or no TV tonight."

But Horrid Henry didn't care. Mother's Day. Oh no. Not again.

Horrid Henry hated Mother's Day.

Last year Peter gave Mum a giant hand-painted card covered in sparkles and glitter which had taken him weeks to make.

Last year Henry also made Mum a card. Okay, so he'd folded over a piece of paper and scrawled "Happy Mother's Day" on it. Was it his fault that the paper he'd picked up off the floor had an advert on the other side for a new kebab shop opening down the road? He'd been busy. He'd made her a card, hadn't he?

Wasn't it the thought that counted?

But no. Mum was never satisfied.

Then Peter bought her a massive bouquet of red roses so Henry picked some tulips from the garden and got told off.

It was so unfair.

Grrr. Aaaarrgh. Why didn't they ever celebrate Children's Day, that's what he wanted to know. Then Mum and Dad

could serve *him* breakfast in bed and buy
him presents and make *him* cards. In fact,
when Henry became King he'd make
it the law that every day was Children's
Day and Mother's Day and Father's
Day would be banned. Any parent
trying to force their child to celebrate
this horrible day would be buried
headfirst in quicksand.

 Naturally, Horrid Henry hadn't bought Mum a present. He'd been so busy watching TV and reading comics and playing on the computer and dragging his weary bones to school and back again that there just hadn't been any time. And Mum and Dad were so mean and horrid and gave him the puniest amount of pocket money ever in the history of the universe so how could he be expected to *buy* a present out of the few measly pence he had rattling round his skeleton bank? He couldn't and that was that. If Mum and Dad wanted presents from him they should give him more cash.

Maybe Mum would forget about Mother's Day, thought Horrid Henry hopefully. She was getting old, after all, and didn't old people forget stuff?

"Well, boys," said Mum, "I'm really looking forward to Mother's Day tomorrow. I can't wait to be pampered like a queen."

"You will be, Mum," said Perfect Peter. "I promise."

Rats.

Rats. Rats. Rats. Rats. Rats.

If only Peter weren't such a goody goody wormy worm toady toad. Once again, Peter would put Henry to shame with his gifts and his cards and running to put a cushion on Mum's chair and making her breakfast in bed and . . .

Wait a minute.

Wait a minute.

Who said Peter had to outdo him this year? What if he, Henry, made Peter look horrid for once? What if, instead of *ignoring* Mother's Day, Henry made tomorrow a Mother's Day Mum would never forget? What if he got Mum a fantastic card and made her the best breakfast in bed ever? In fact, if he *bought* a card, it would be much better than any home-made monstrosity Peter had painted.

And, if he got up super early, he could

have Mum's breakfast all ready while
Peter was still snoozing. Ha! That would
be the best trick ever. Henry couldn't
wait to see Peter's shocked face when
Peter brought up Mum's breakfast tray
to find her already tucking into Henry's
yummalicious treats.

"I've got a big surprise planned for
you," said Perfect Peter.

"How exciting," said Mum, beaming.

"After all, you are the best mum in the
world," said Peter.

"Thank you, Peter," said Mum.

Anything Peter could say, Henry
could say better.

"Actually," said Henry,
"I think you're the best
mum in the universe."

Mum smiled. "Why,
thank you, Henry," she
said.

"You're the best mum who's ever lived," said Peter.

"You're the best mum who's ever lived and will ever live," said Henry.

Peter opened his mouth and then closed it. He couldn't think of anything to say to top that.

"Just wait till you see all the presents I've got you, Mum," said Peter. "How many do you have, Henry?"

"None of your business, worm," said Henry. He glanced at the clock. Yikes.  He only had fifteen minutes before the corner shop closed. Never mind. It was sure to be filled with fabulous Mother's Day cards and gifts.

"Be right back," shouted Horrid Henry.

Henry stood in front of the Mother's Day card display. The shelf was empty.

There wasn't a single Mother's Day card left.

How could there be no more cards?

His brilliant plan was ruined before he'd even started.

He had to find a card. If it just said, "Best wishes" then he could write "Happy Mother's Day" on the inside. Yikes, every card in this stupid shop cost so much. Who knew cards were so expensive?

Wait. There was a plastic box in the corner filled with cards.

ANY CARD 50 PENCE read the sign. It was his lucky day!

Henry ran over and riffled through them.

Sorry about your hernia

Sorry you're leaving

Happy 90th birthday
That'll do, thought
Horrid Henry,
grabbing the card.
He'd cross out the *90th*
and *birth* and write in
Mother's instead.

She'll never notice,
thought Horrid Henry.

Now, some presents.
What would Mum
like?

Horrid Henry
wandered up the aisles.

Horrid Henry
wandered down the

aisles. He had three minutes left before
closing time to find the best Mother's
Day gifts ever.

What about a new toilet brush? This
pearly white one came with a selection

81

of cleaning supplies! And
matching toilet roll holder.
What a fantastic present. Mum
would be sure to love it.

On the other hand, it cost
£4.99. £4.99? Highway
robbery. He'd already spent
50p. And he had comics to buy.
He wasn't made of money.

What about a DVD, *Beat Your Blubber*?
Rats, even that was £1.99. If he bought
it he'd have
no money left
for sweets
this month.
Besides,
Mum didn't
have much
blubber to
beat.
Maybe

Growing Old Gracefully would be better.

Aha. How about that book for 25p, *Hello Dentures*. The price was right, thought Horrid Henry, grabbing it. And he'd have cash left over for chocolate for him!

Hang on. What was Mum saying she needed just the other day? A new mop. Yes! She'd been moaning and moaning

that the old one was falling apart. She'd love a new mop.

Actually, they were expensive. Rats. Why did everything cost so much? Wait. He was a genius. He'd just cut a rag into strips and then use a rubber band to attach them to the old mop handle. Voilà! A brand new mop. What mother wouldn't love such a great gift?

What a lucky mum she was, thought Horrid Henry, as he strolled home with his book and card. Now all he had to do was to dream up a few more fantastic gifts tonight, and Mother's Day was sorted. Peter was toast.

Horrid Henry sat in his bedroom. He'd made the mop. What else could he give Mum?

Why not make her some coupons? Genius.

Another great gift for Mother's Day, and, even better, it wouldn't cost him a penny. Horrid Henry got out some paper and crayons, and wrote:

THIS MOTHERS DAY COUPON IS GOOD FOR _____

What did mums like doing best of all? Cleaning up after their children! After all, Mum was lucky to have him for her child. She could have got someone really awful, like Weepy William or Stuck-Up Steve. In fact, anyone else, really. Henry shuddered. Mum didn't know how lucky she was, having Henry for her son.

Horrid Henry filled in the coupon.

THIS MOTHERS DAY COUPON IS GOOD FOR _____
Cleaning Henry's room

THIS MOTHERS
DAY COUPON
IS GOOD FOR
*Cleaning
Henry's room*
Henry

That was sure
to make her
happy. In fact,
why not be
generous, and
give her a pack
of ten?

There was a
knock on his
door.

"All ready for
Mother's Day?" asked Peter.

"Of course," said Henry smoothly.
"I've got Mum loads of presents and
I'm making her breakfast in bed."

Perfect Peter stood still.

"But that's *my* surprise," said Peter.
"*I'm* making her breakfast in bed."

Horrid Henry smiled.

"Tough," he said.

Peter glared at Henry.

Henry glared at Peter.

Ha, thought Horrid Henry. He'd get up super early to make sure he got Mum's breakfast ready first. He'd do soft-boiled eggs, toast, jam, juice, tea – the works.

Tee hee Peter, thought Horrid Henry. If you snooze, you lose.

Clink. Clink. Clunk. Clunk.

Horrid Henry opened one eye. It was still dark outside. Who could be moving about the kitchen making so much noise so early?

Then Horrid Henry sat up. Peter! That little ratty toad. He'd got up early to beat Henry.

Well, not so fast.

Henry bolted out of bed and dashed into the kitchen.

There was Peter bustling around,

getting out napkins and cutlery on a tray
decorated with a red rose.

"Whatcha doin', worm?"

"Making Mum her Mother's Day
breakfast in bed," said Peter, placing two
pieces of toast in the toaster.

"Glad someone is," said Henry,
yawning.

Peter paused.

"Aren't you making her breakfast, Henry?" asked Peter.

"Nah," said Henry. "You go ahead."

Then Henry cocked his head and went to the door.

"Peter, Dad's calling you."

"I didn't hear anything," said Peter.

"Okay, I'll go," said Henry. "He said it was about Mother's Day . . ."

Peter shot out of the kitchen and dashed upstairs.

Henry nipped to the toaster.

Zip!

Peter's toast was out and in the bin.

Pop!

Horrid Henry put in FOUR pieces of toast, then stood guard.

Perfect Peter dashed back into the kitchen.

"Dad didn't call me," said Peter. "He was asleep."

"Yeah he did," said Henry.

"No, he – where's the toast I was making Mum?" said Peter.

Henry ignored him.

"Where's Mum's toast?" said Peter.

"What toast?" said Henry.

"You took my toast out of the toaster!"

"Didn't."

"Did."

"Didn't."

"Liar."

"Liar."

Slap!

Slap!

"Mum!" screamed Henry and Peter.

"Henry slapped me," yelled Peter.

"Peter slapped me first," yelled Henry.

"Didn't!"

"Did!"

"Liar!"

"Liar!"

Dad stumbled in just as Henry pulled
Peter's hair.

Peter started screaming.

"Henry! Leave your brother alone," he shouted. "It's Mother's Day."

"I'm making her breakfast in bed, and then Peter came in and tried to steal my toast," said Henry.

Peter gasped.

"I was making her toast first," he wailed. "Henry's lying."

Dad sighed.

"Why don't you *both* make her breakfast in bed?" he said, yawning and stumbling back upstairs.

Henry looked at Peter.

Peter looked at Henry.

"Sure, Dad," said Horrid Henry.

Henry raced to the toaster, yanked out the toast and threw it on a red tray. No time for a plate. Or butter.

Now for the eggs.

Peter snatched the jam and put it on *his* tray, then poured some juice and got out the cereal.

Oh no. Peter was getting ahead of him! He'd be first upstairs with his breakfast, and all Henry's hard work would be for nothing. Henry dashed to the fridge, snatched two eggs and flung them into egg cups. No time to soft-boil them.

Anyway, they'd just be a bit runnier than normal, right?

Henry frantically poured orange juice into a glass and ran to the door with his tray. Forget the tea. Peter pounded after him, clutching his breakfast tray.

Henry shoved his tray in front of Peter, blocking him, then galloped up the stairs.

Victory!

"Happy Mother's Day," screamed Horrid Henry, bursting into Mum and Dad's bedroom.

"Happy Mother's Day," screamed Perfect Peter, jostling Henry as he burst into the room.

"Huunhn," grunted Mum.

Henry tried to shove Peter out of the way with his tray.

Peter tried to shove Henry out of the way with his tray.

Slosh!

Juice went all over Henry's tray and spilled over Mum.

Cereal went all over Peter's tray and spilled over Mum.

Smash!

Crash!

Mum was covered in runny raw egg, broken shells, juice and cereal.

"Yum," she said faintly.

"Don't worry, Mum," yelled Horrid Henry. "I've got just the perfect present to mop you up!"

Visit my wicked website
www.horridhenry.co.uk
for jokes, book news,
competitions and more!

Don't forget
to sign up for my
newsletter while
you're there!

www.horridhenry.co.uk

Collect all the
Horrid Henry storybooks!

Horrid Henry

Horrid Henry
and the Secret Club

Horrid Henry Tricks
the Tooth Fairy

Horrid Henry
Gets Rich Quick

Horrid Henry's Nits

Horrid Henry's
Haunted House

Horrid Henry and
the Mummy's Curse

Horrid Henry's
Revenge

Horrid Henry and the
Bogey Babysitter

Horrid Henry's Stinkbomb

HORRID HENRY
and the Zombie Vampire

Horrid Henry terrorizes his classmates at a
school sleepover in the museum, plays with
Perfect Peter and tricks him into handing over
all his money, gets out of writing his own story
for Miss Battle-Axe by adapting one of Peter's,
and meets the Nudie Foodie, a celebrity chef,
who comes to the school to improve
school dinners. No more burgers!
No more chips!

HORRID HENRY'S
Monster Movie

Horrid Henry makes his own scary movie,
persuades Peter to hand over his stash of
Grump Cards and spends a weekend at Aunt
Ruby's where he has to share a bedroom with
his two arch-enemies, Stuck-Up Steve and
Bossy Bill. Then when Henry's school decides
to have a mini-Olympics, he sets up his
own Holympics, with medals for
crisp-eating, TV watching, and
Burping to the Beat.

the orion star

Sign up for **the orion star** newsletter
for all the latest children's book news,
plus activity sheets, exclusive competitions,
author interviews, pre-publication extracts
and more.

www.orionbooks.co.uk/newsletters

Follow @the_orionstar on .

Orion
Children's Books